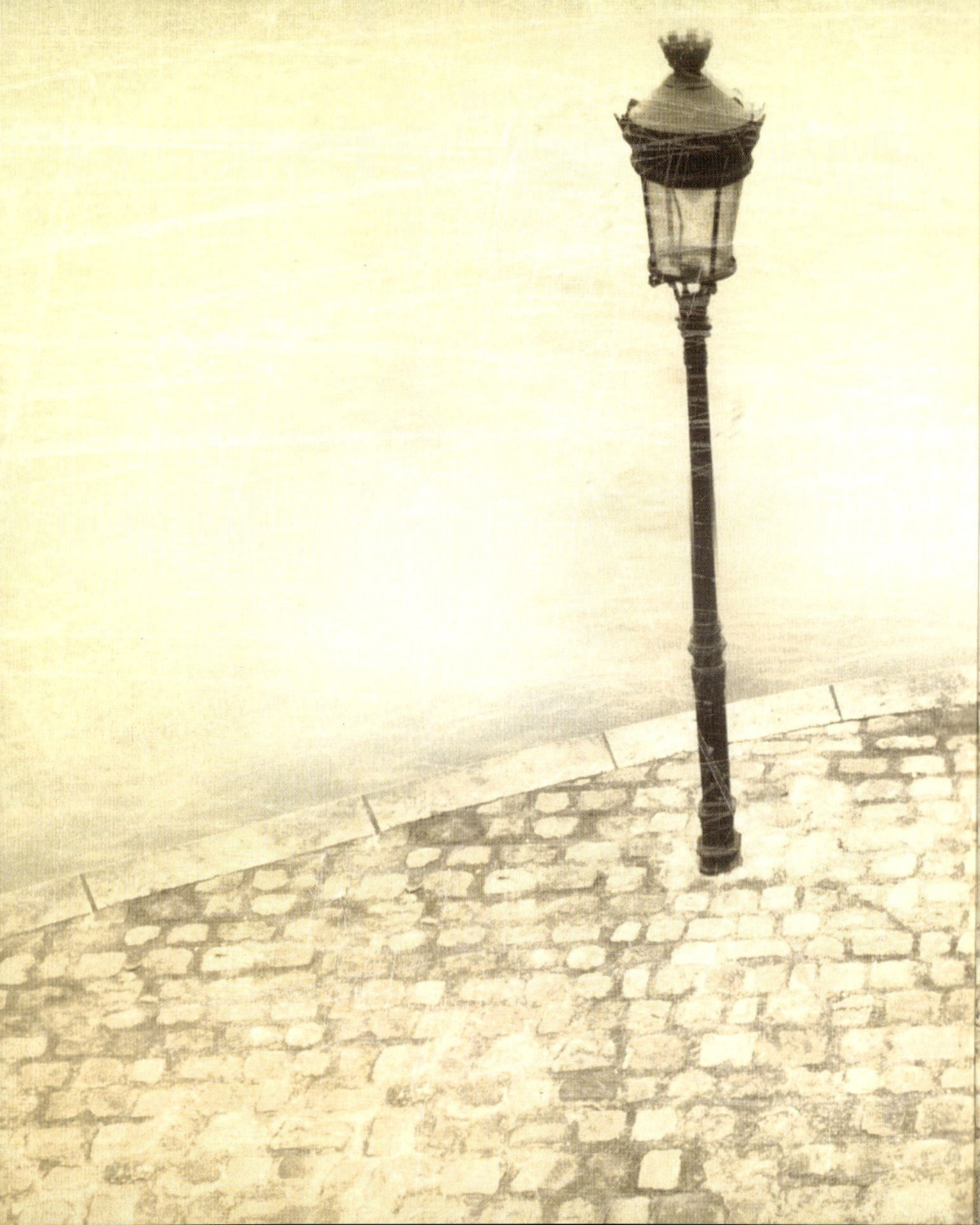

Dance
WHILE YOU CAN

Gentle Reminders to Help You Live Life to the Fullest

LANCE WUBBELS

GIFT BOOKS
from Hallmark

INTRODUCTION

First I was dying to finish high school and start college.

And then I was dying to finish college and start working.

And then I was dying to marry and have children.

And then I was dying for my children

    to grow old enough

so I could get back to my career.

And then I was dying to retire.

And now I am dying . . .

    and suddenly realize that I forgot to live.

AUTHOR UNKNOWN

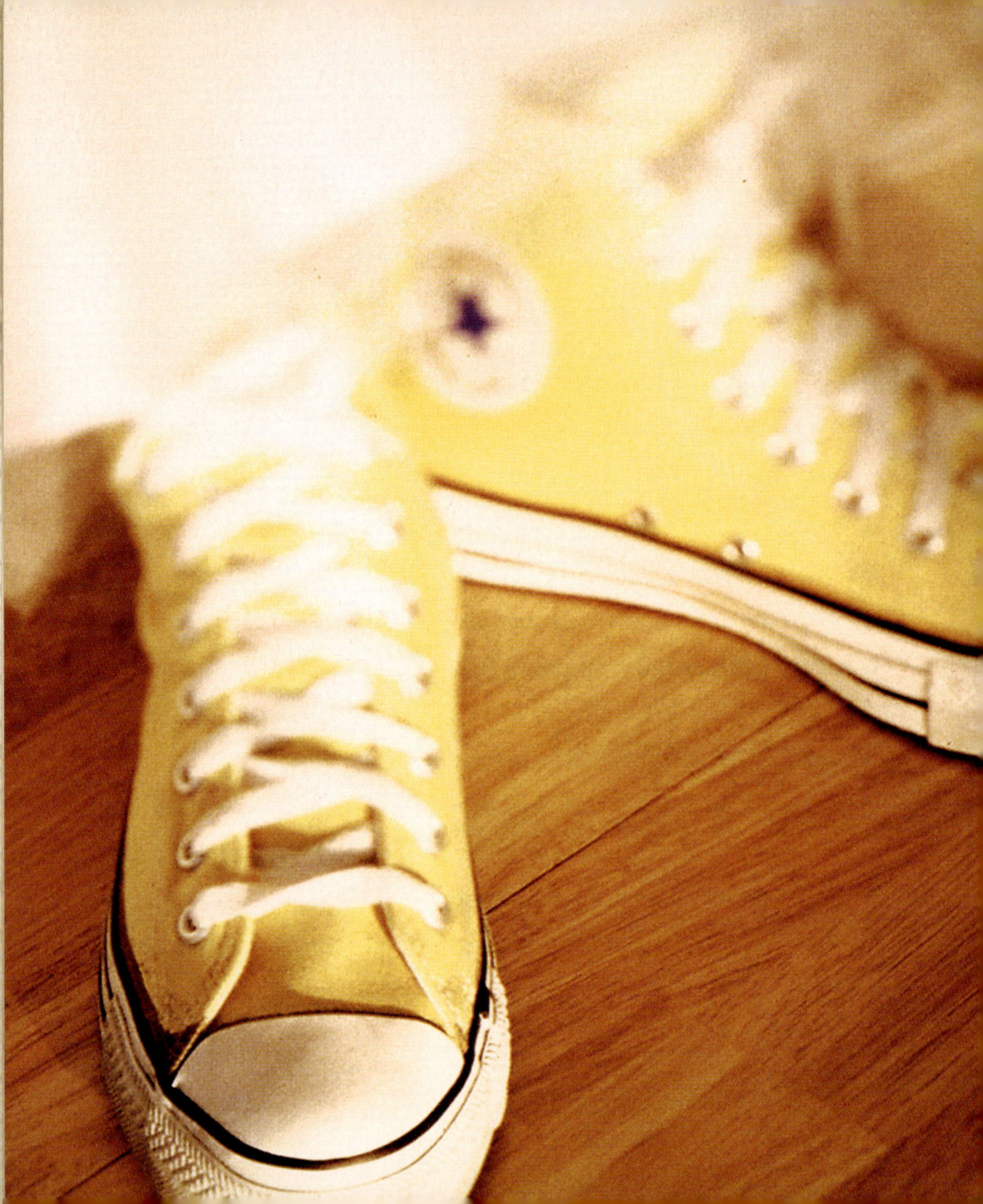

Dance While You Can . . .

I WILL NOT STAND TO THE SIDE

AND ALLOW THE MUSIC IN MY HEART

TO FADE AWAY AND DIE.

I WILL DANCE TO MY OWN LIFE SONG.

While I Still Can Dance . . .

I want to dance with my loved ones . . .

to watch our dreams unfold,

one by one.

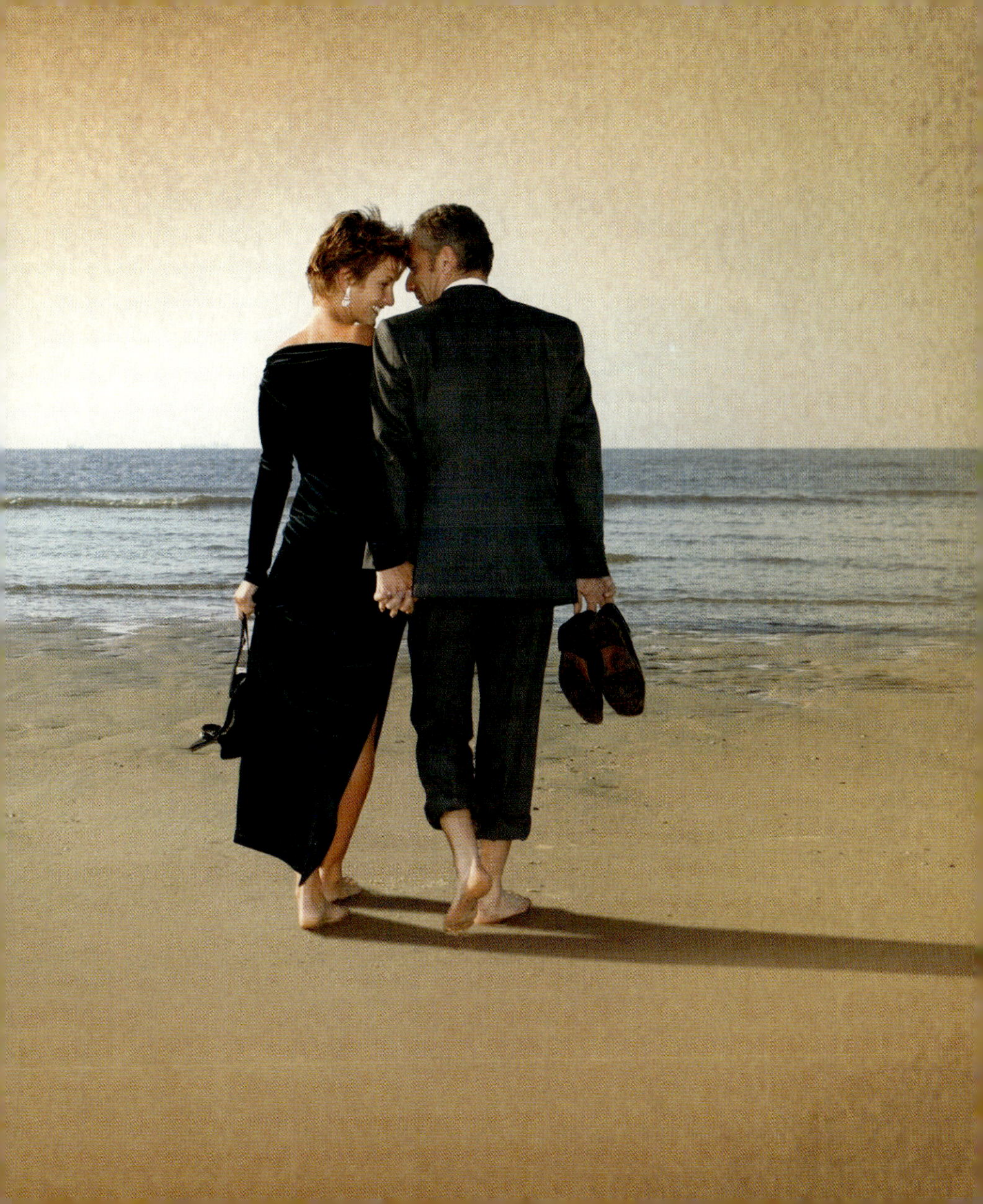

TO DANCE . . .

I will stop looking back

WITH REGRETS . . .

or looking forward

WITH FEAR . . .

and give the best I have today.

Dance While You Can . . .

    I will quiet my soul . . .

    silence the noise in my head and heart . . .

    and ask myself

    what I really want out of life.

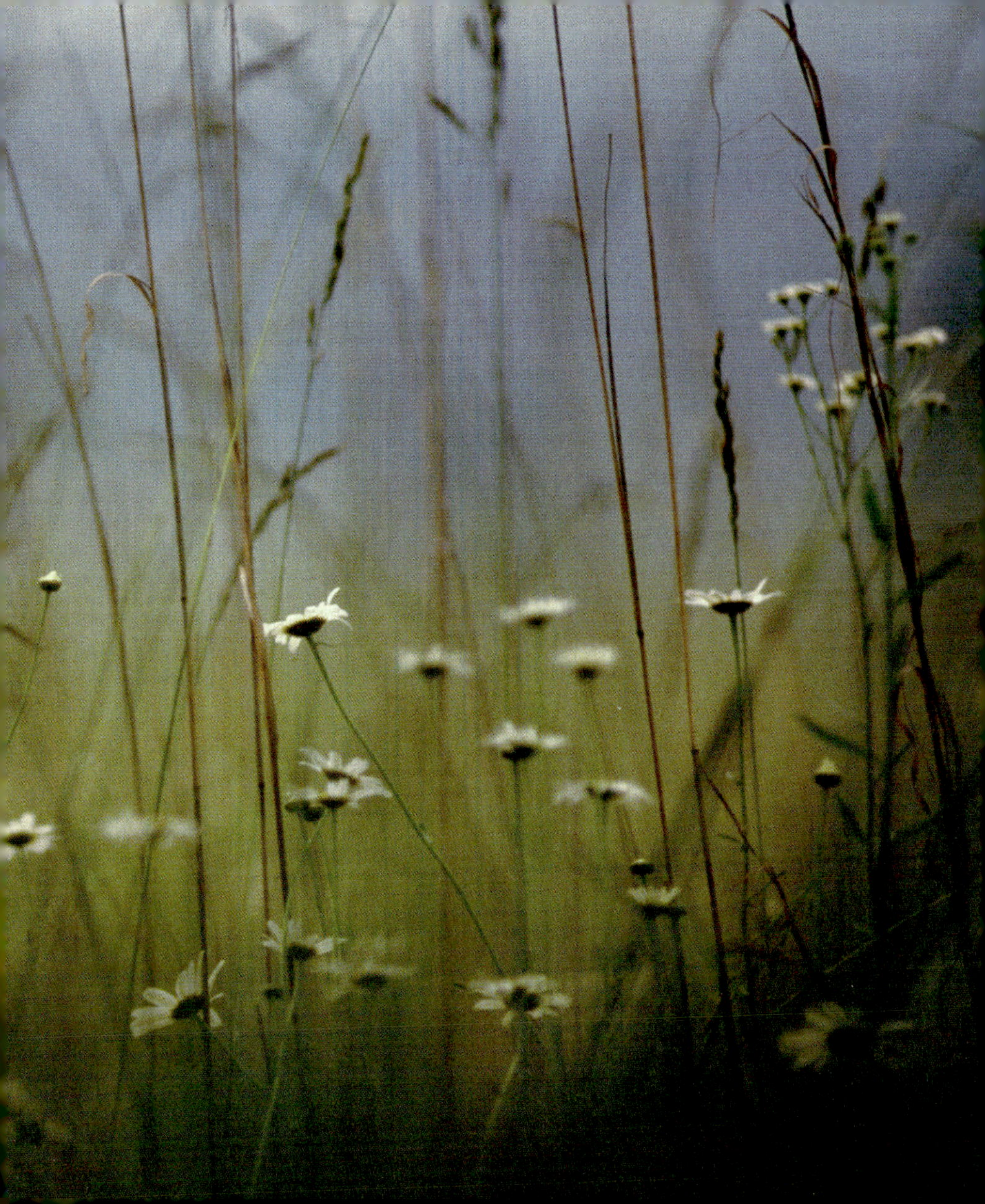

WHILE I STILL CAN DANCE . . .

I will sing of the joy

I've found in you.

Being with you

chases the rest of the world away.

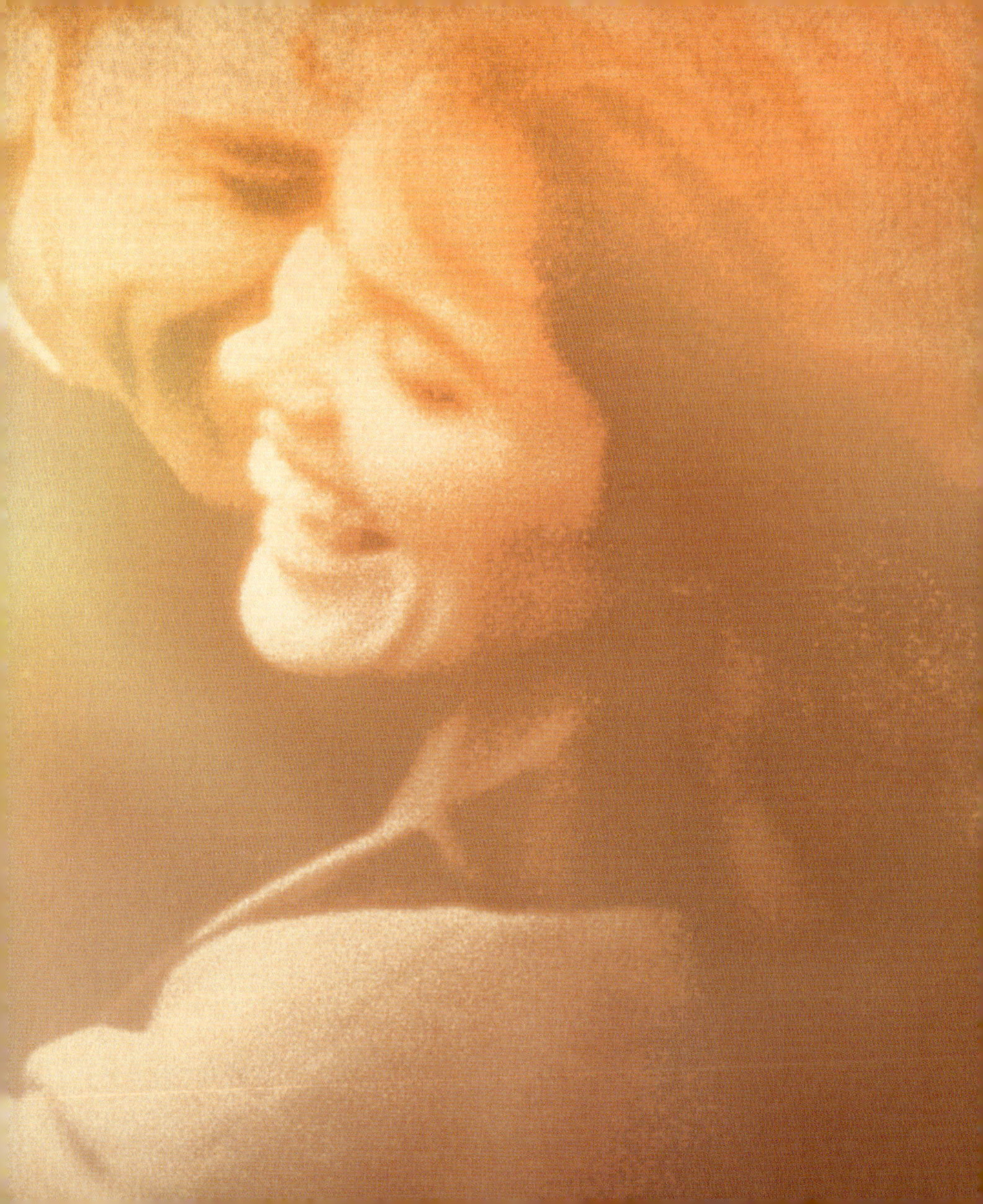

To Dance . . .

I WILL SLOW DOWN,

SET LIMITS ON MY COMMITMENTS AND WORK,

    AND MAKE CERTAIN THAT THOSE WHOM I LOVE

    REMAIN FIRST IN MY LIFE.

    I will not allow the pressures that bear down

        upon our lives to get wedged

        between us and keep us apart.

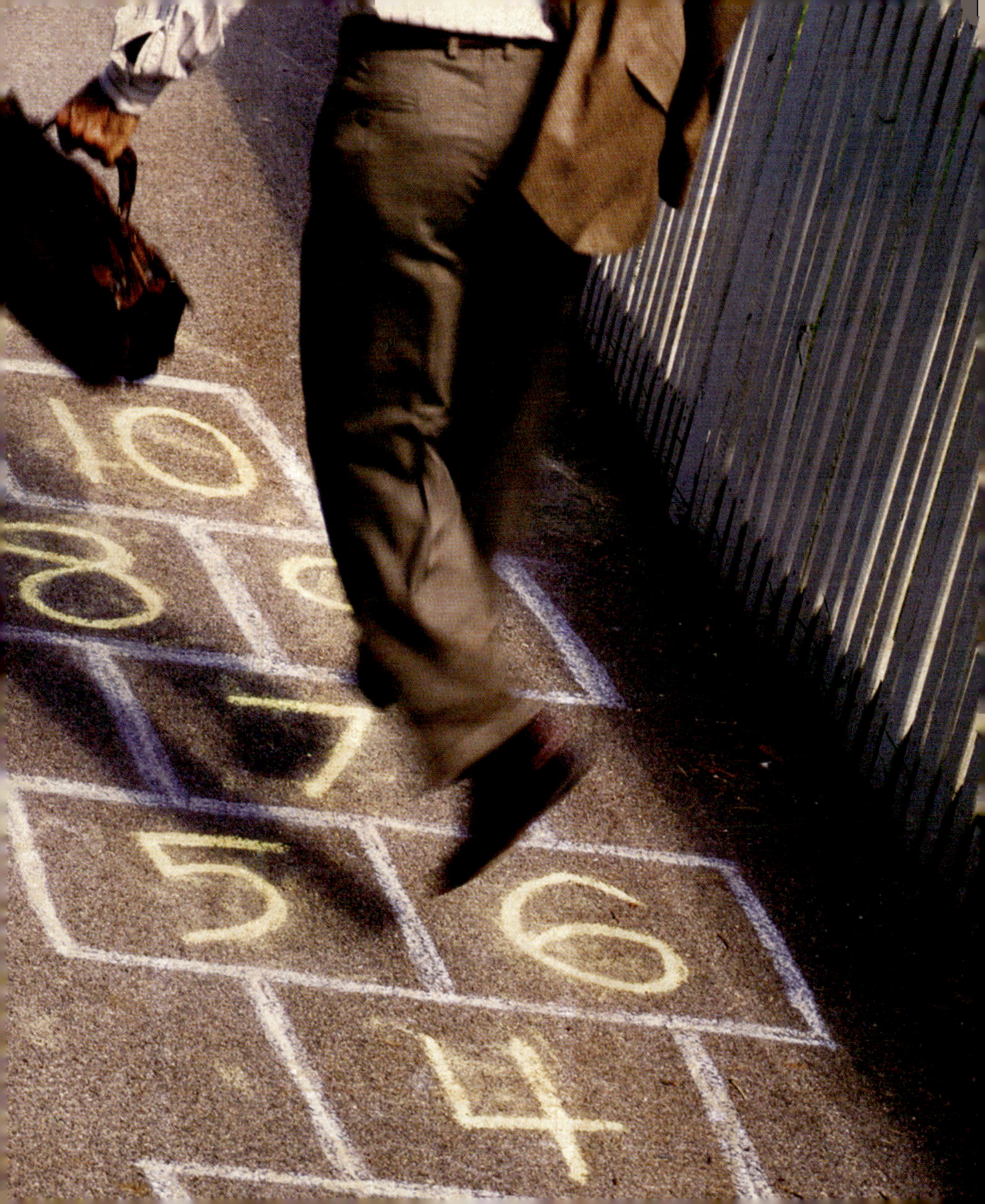
10
8
7
5
6
4

DANCE WHILE YOU CAN . . .

I will make a commitment to fulfilling my dreams . . .

no matter what I may be feeling . . .

and I will dare to move forward

in the face of life's challenges.

I will believe that what God has placed inside me is superior to the mountains that stand in my way.

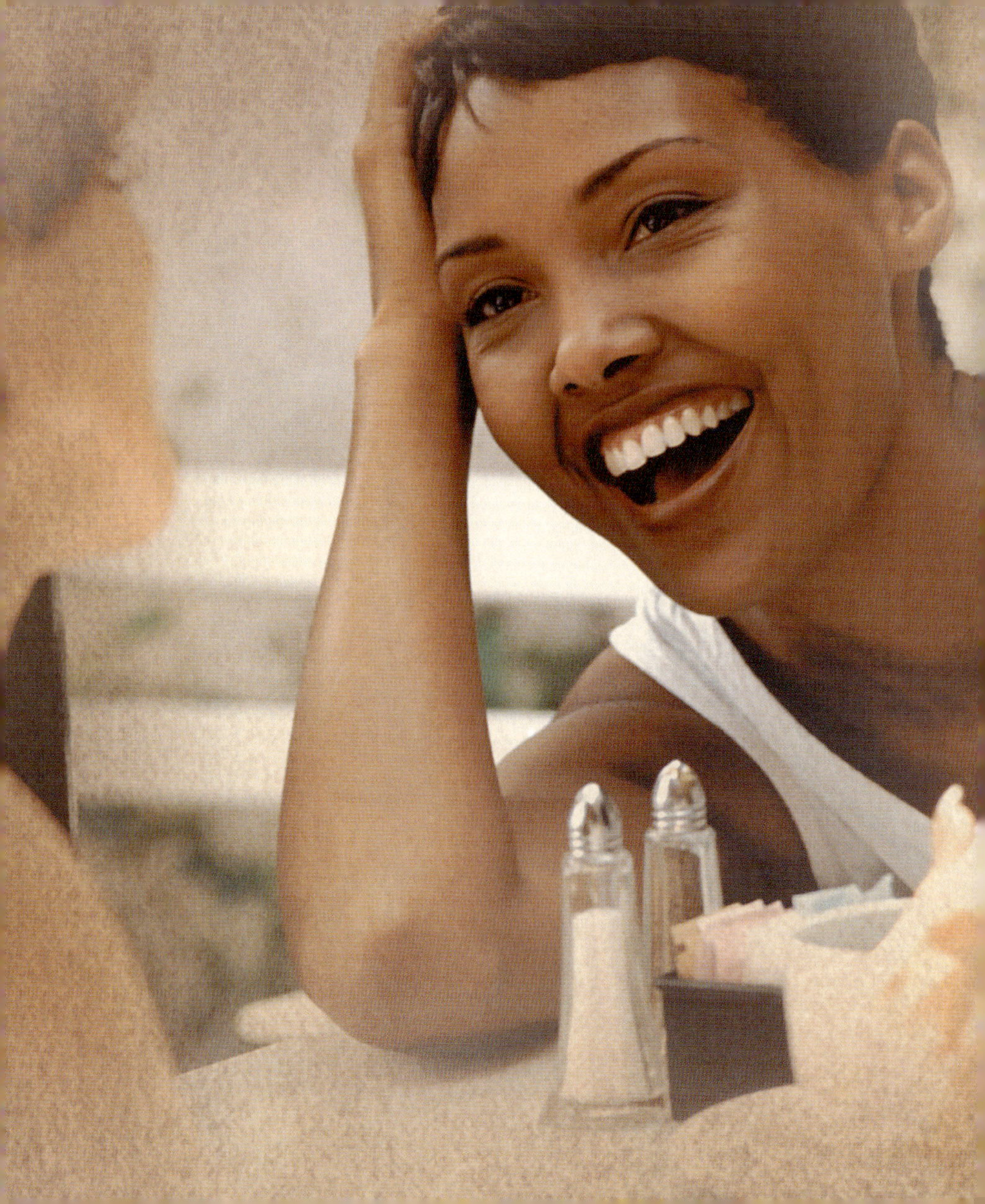

WHILE I STILL CAN DANCE . . .

I will look loved ones in the eyes,

take their hands in mine,

and tell them how much I love them.

I will make the most of our time together.

To Dance . . .

I WILL TAKE RESPONSIBILITY

    for my reactions to people

    and stop blaming others for how I am feeling.

I WILL KEEP SILENT

    when the opportunity comes

    to talk behind someone else's back.

DANCE WHILE YOU CAN . . .

I will listen to more than the words
being spoken to me . . .
listen for the heart expression . . .
search out their meaning,
and then speak from my own heart.

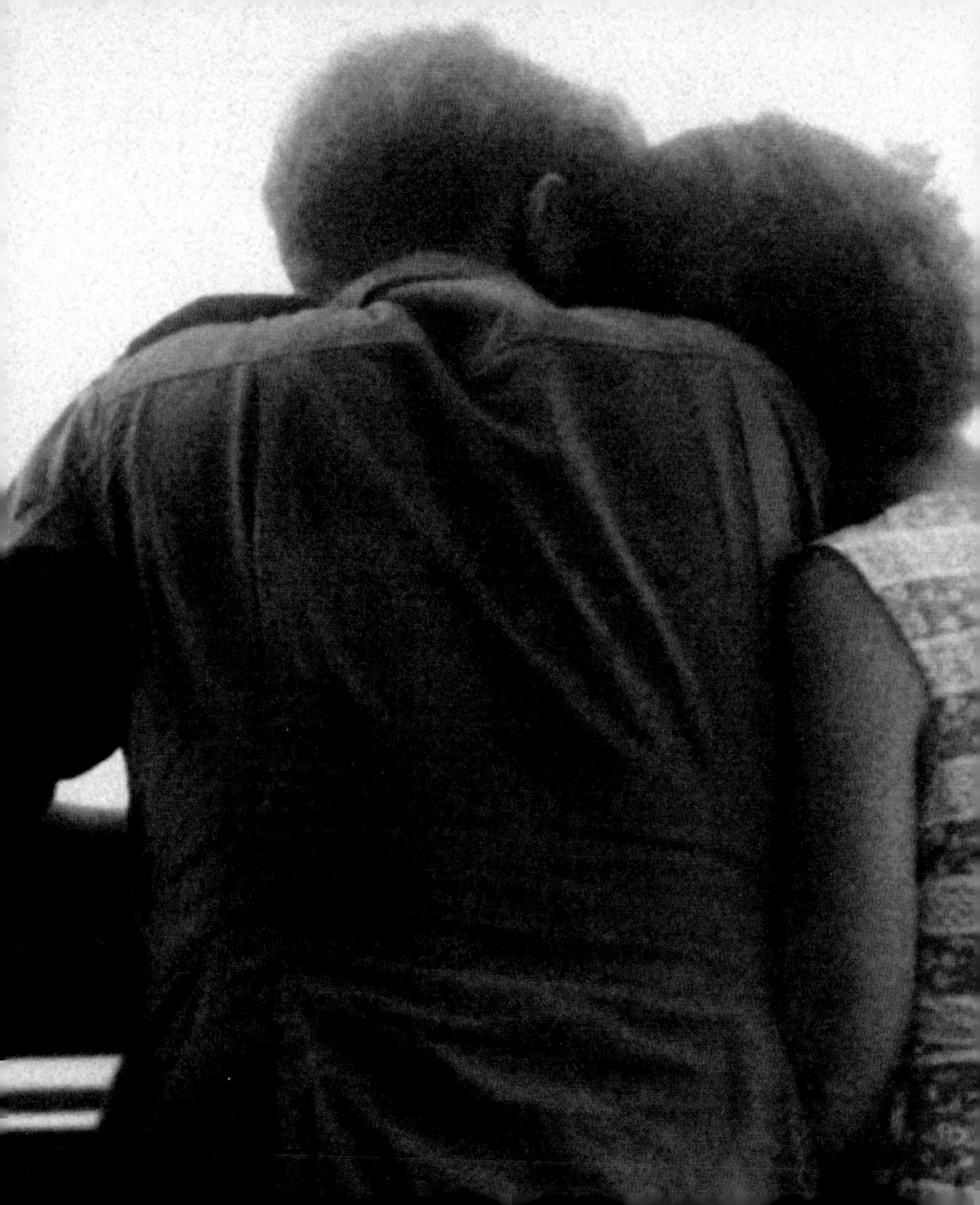

WHILE I STILL CAN DANCE . . .

I will hold my loved ones tight
and hope to never let them go.
How could I dance without them?

Dance While You Can . . .

I will believe I was born to dance . . .

created by God to make a difference

in people's lives.

I will call my friends . . .

just to talk . . .

just to let them know I care

and that I'm thankful

for the joy they've brought me.

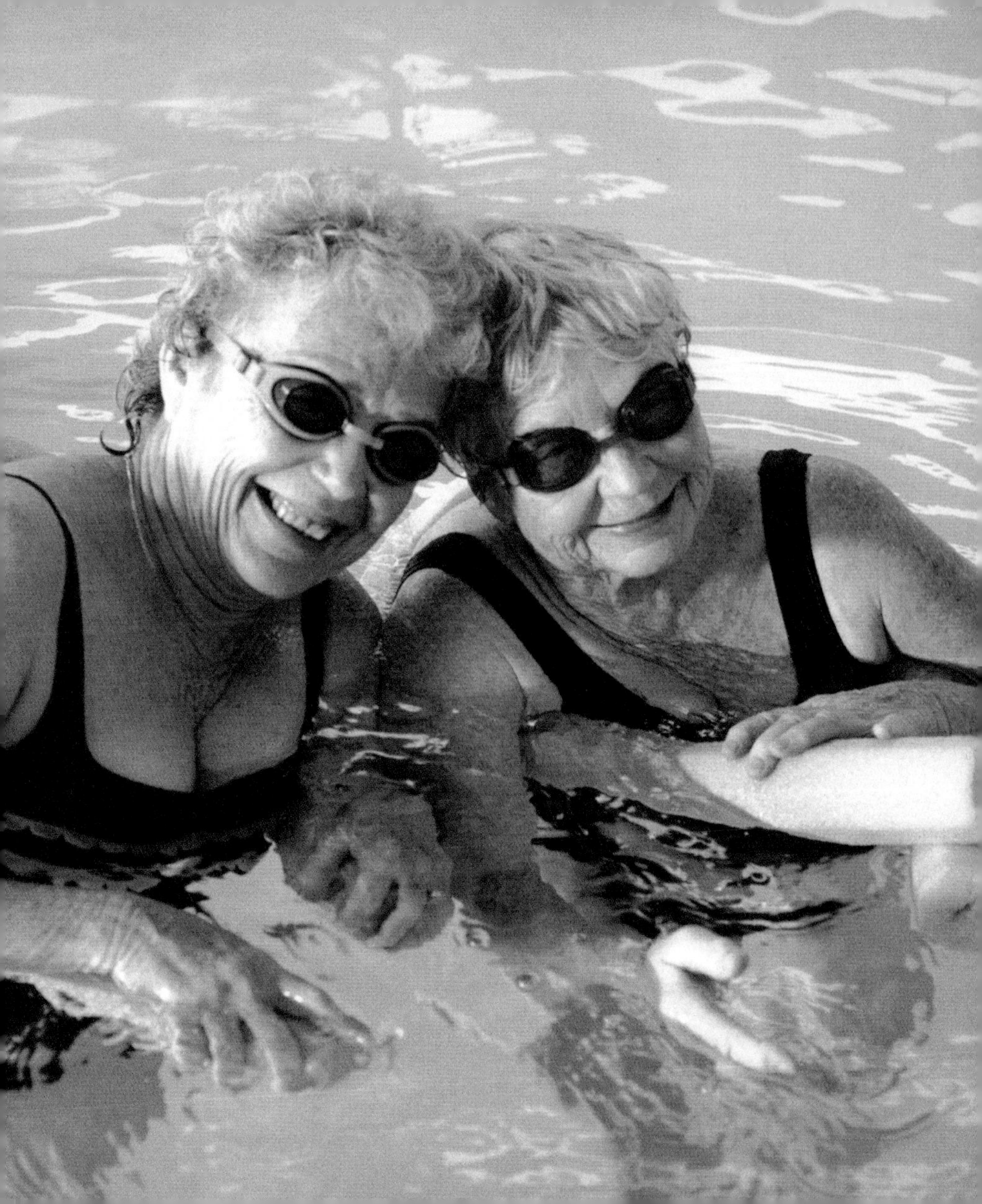

While I Still Can Dance . . .

I will always treat others with dignity,

honor, and respect.

I will keep secrets secret

and guard others' privacy.

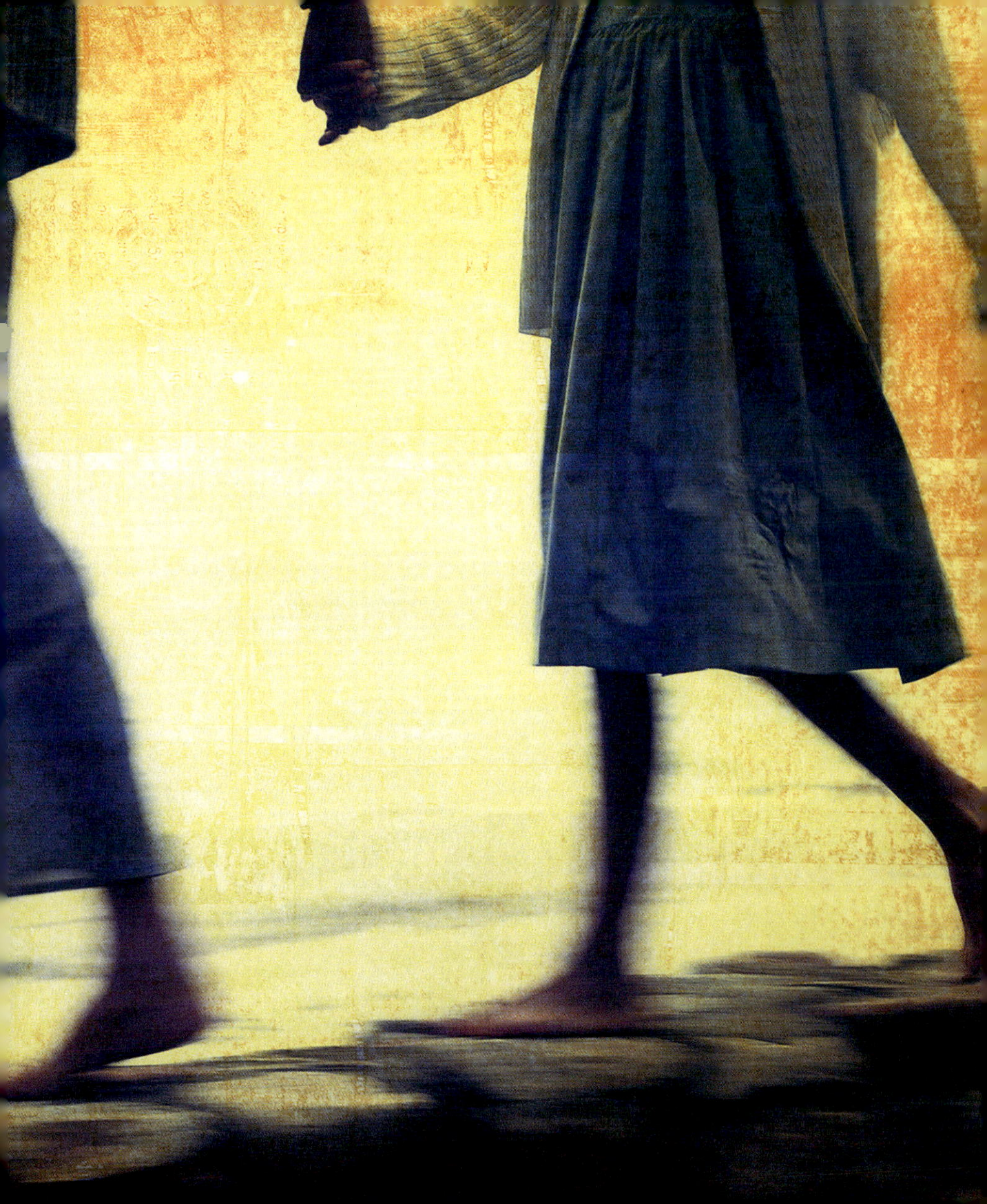

TO DANCE . . .

I will stop doing things the same old way
just because I like to play it safe.

I will be daring and courageous
and refuse to allow fear to control my actions.

While I Still Can Dance . . .

I WILL SHARE YOUR HOPES

AND DREAMS AND DESIRES.

I WILL BELIEVE

THAT YOU CAN TURN YOUR DREAMS

INTO REALITY.

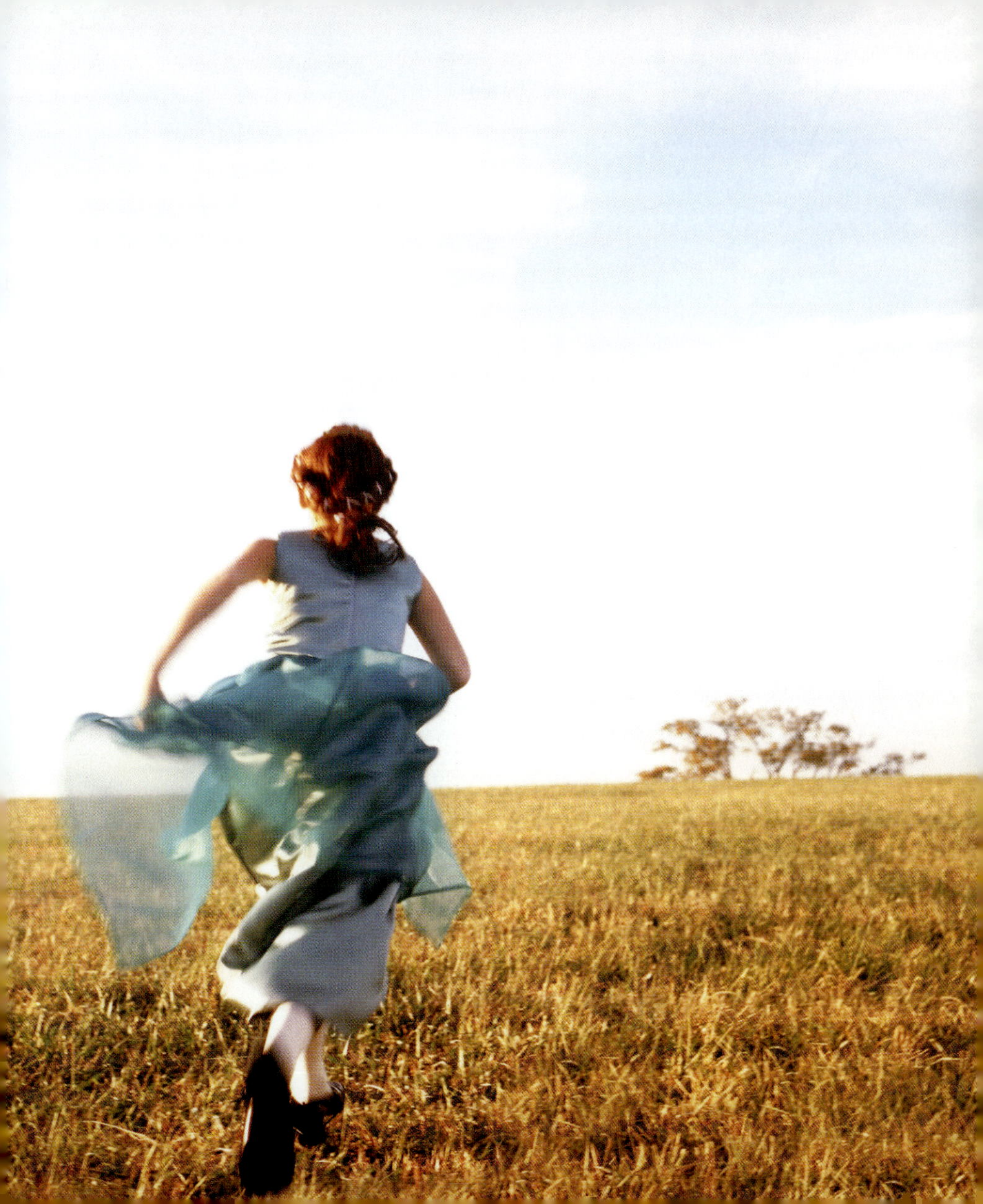

Dance While You Can . . .

I WILL CELEBRATE

THE SHEER JOY OF BEING ALIVE . . .

THE JOY OF BEING CREATED

IN THE IMAGE OF GOD.

I will not be cheated out of enjoying life's pleasures—

the people I meet, the food I eat,

the sunshine in the trees,

the company of a friend.

WHILE I STILL CAN DANCE . . .

        I will make certain my loved ones

        know how precious they are to me.

        I will serve them with my whole heart . . .

            with joy and freedom.

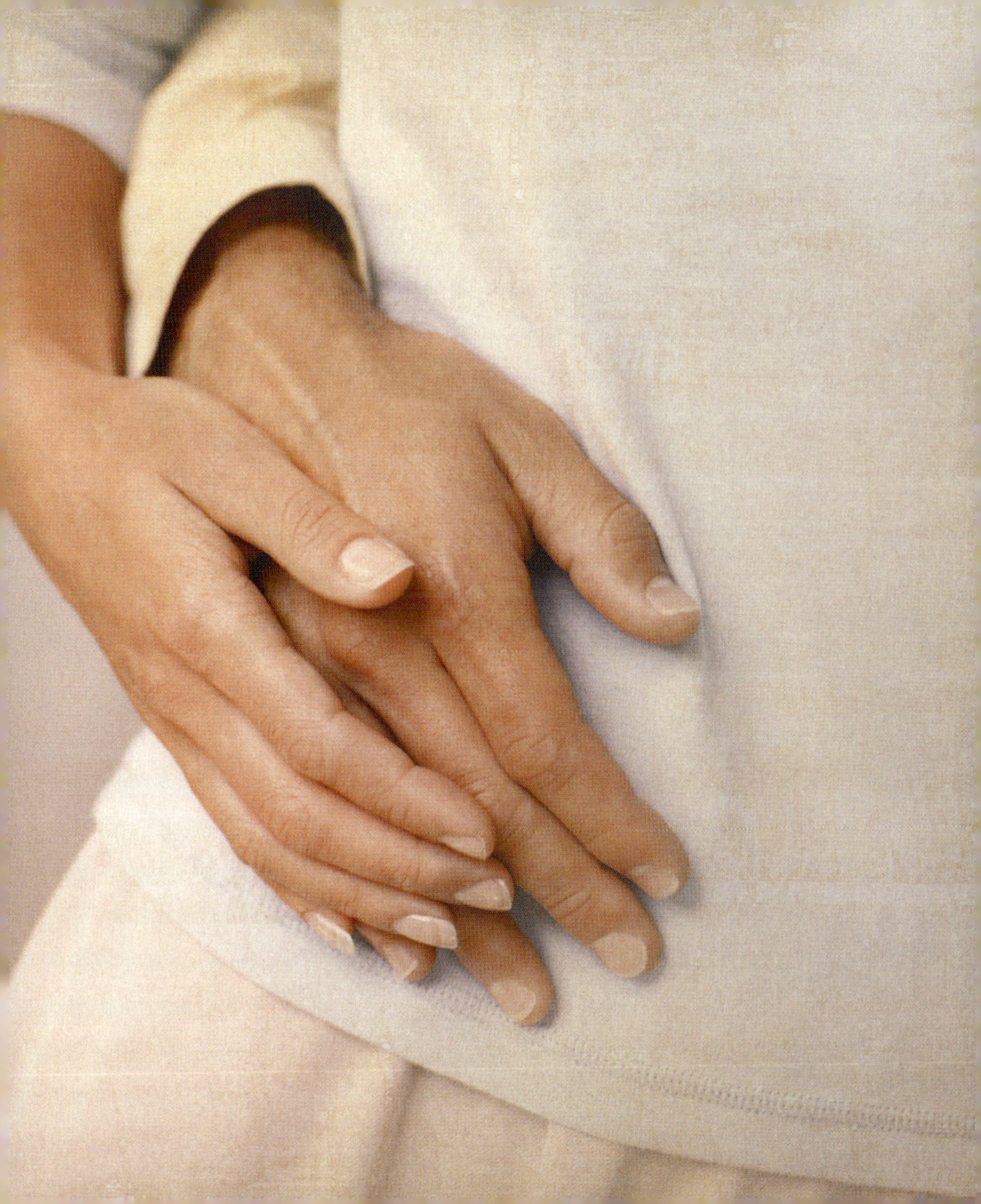

TO DANCE . . .

I will be faithful to keep my promises,

even the ones that cost me dearly.

May my word

or even a nod be enough.

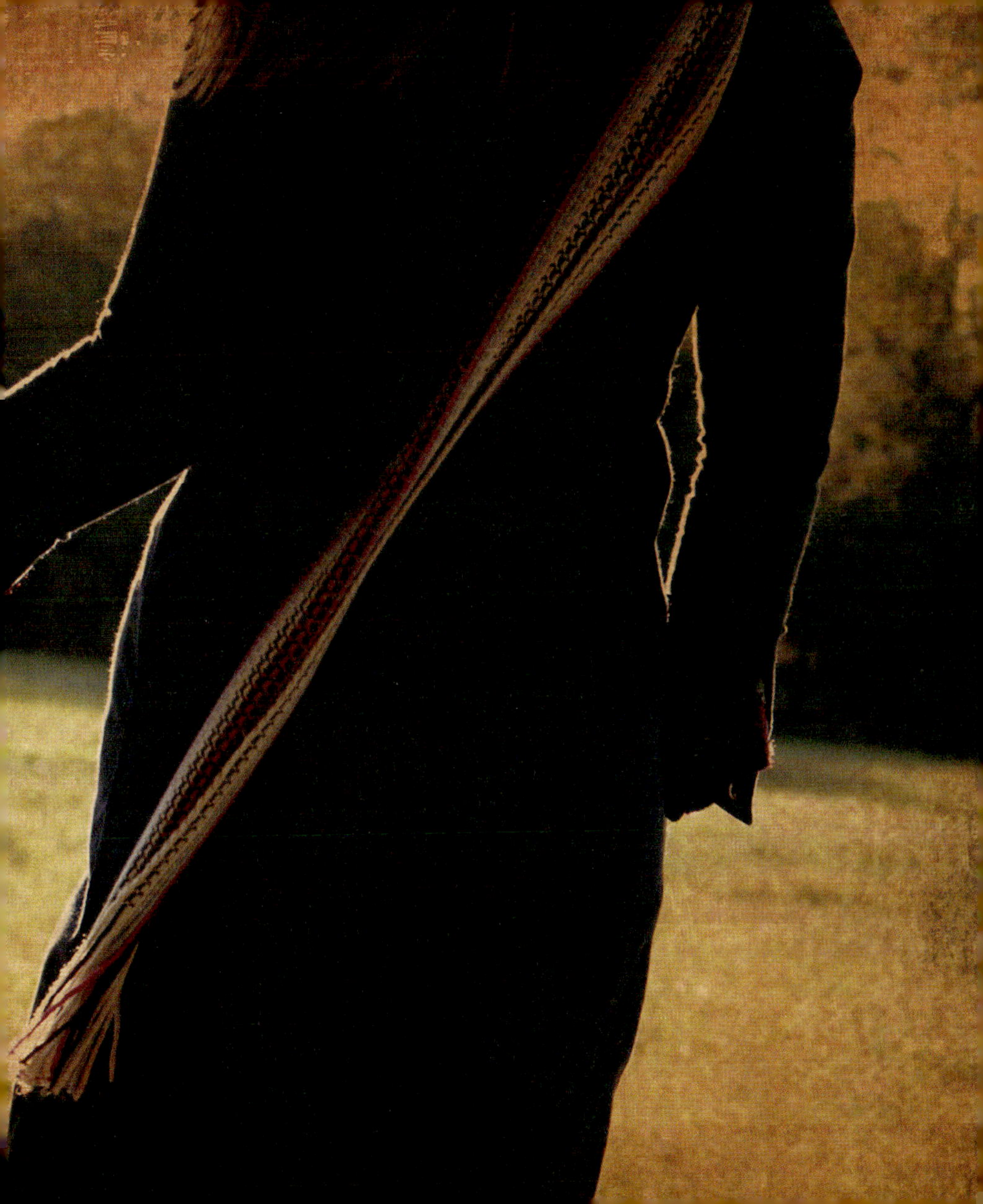

While I Still Can Dance . . .

I will get rid of any

      BITTERNESS

      or RESENTMENT

      or ANGER in my life.

I will FORGIVE others and not waste my life

      trying to settle scores.

I will APOLOGIZE to others for anything

      I've done or said that was wrong.

Dance While You Can . . .

I WILL REFUSE TO DANCE

TO THE PRESSURE

TO BE OR TO DO

OR TO PROVE SOMETHING

IN ORDER TO WIN SOMEONE'S LOVE

OR ACCEPTANCE.

I AM NOT A SLAVE TO THE OPINIONS OF OTHERS.

WHILE I STILL CAN DANCE . . .

I will dare to open

the vaults of my heart and mind

and express my feelings for others.

And I welcome others

to share their hearts

and minds with me.

TO DANCE . . .

I will let the love of God

touch the depths of my heart

and mold me into the person I should be.

I will make love the center

of my being and all I do.

While I Still Can Dance . . .

    I will celebrate the relationships I share

    and never take them for granted.

    I will treasure them

        as one of life's sweetest joys.

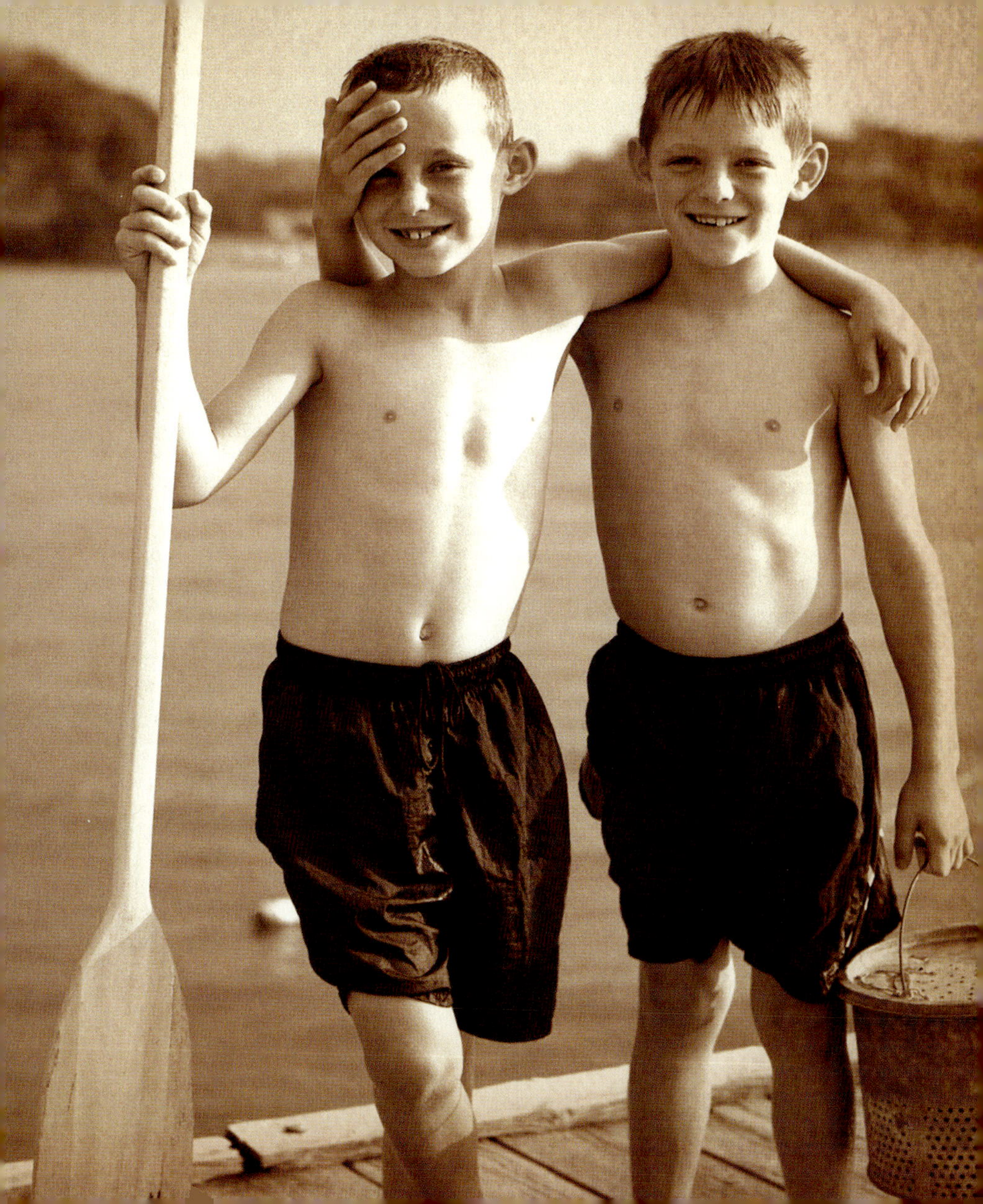

DANCE WHILE YOU CAN . . .

I will make truth the hallmark of my life.

I will have the courage

    to make decisions

    that I stand behind without wavering.

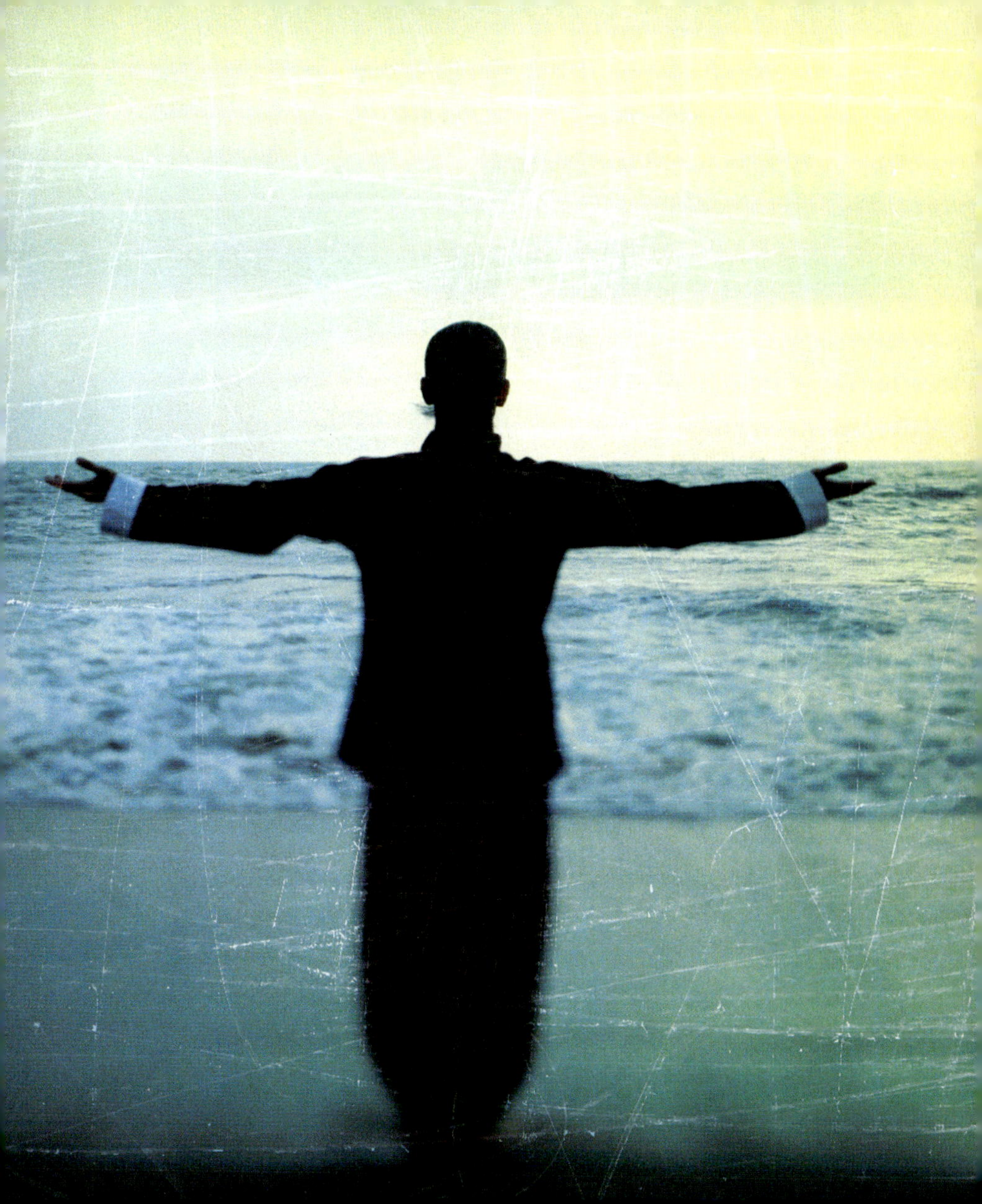

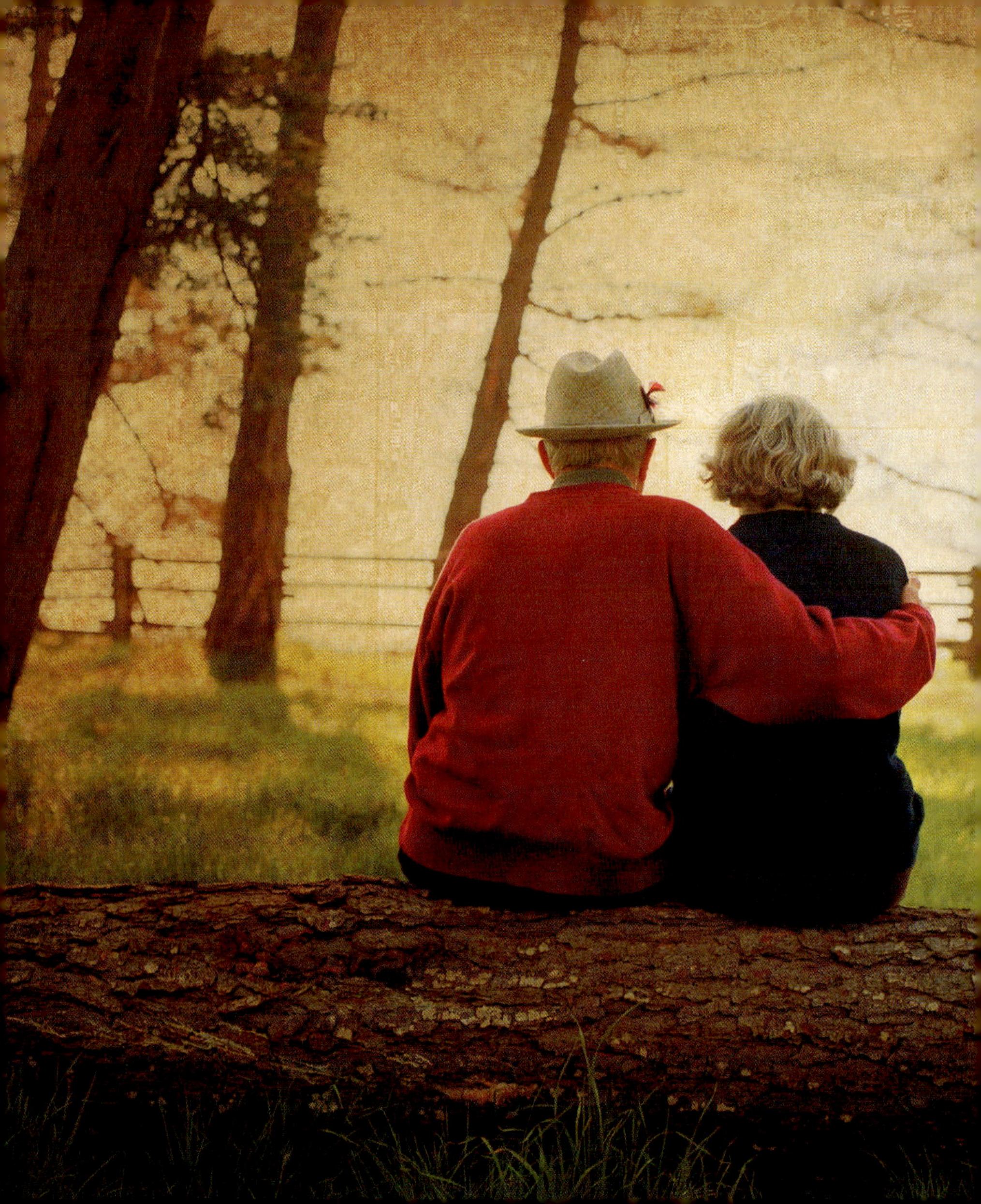

While I Still Can Dance . . .

I will take pleasure in the smiles that warm me

and in the hugs

that always say "I love you."

To Dance . . .

I WILL STOP COMPLAINING ABOUT WHAT I DON'T HAVE,

AND I WILL LEARN TO BE TRULY GRATEFUL

FOR WHAT I DO HAVE.

I WILL BE CONTENT,

THOUGH NOT COMPLACENT.

Dance While You Can . . .

I will take every new day as a fresh beginning in God's grace and allow my world to be made new.

I will savor the beauty and wonder of the world around me.

While I Still Can Dance . . .

    I will love others just the way they are . . .

without judging them or trying

to change them into the image of what

I'd like them to become.

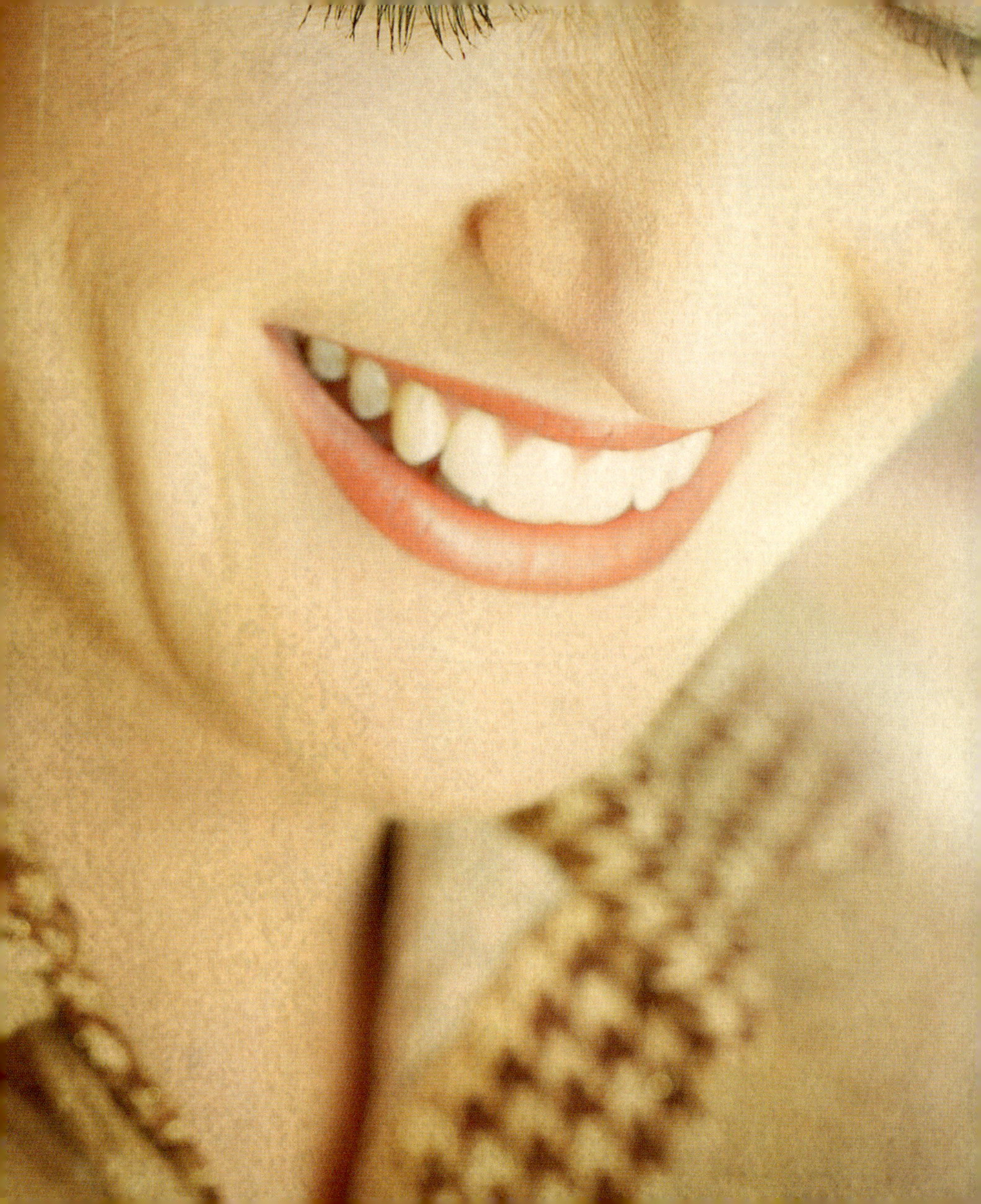

To Dance . . .

    I will stop getting upset

    when things go wrong

    and my world is not what

    I want it to be.

    I will find joy in life's challenges

    and risks and hopes.

DANCE WHILE YOU CAN . . .

I refuse to allow my past to determine my future.

I will not let past disappointments

with my parents or spouse

or boss or anything,

whether it's my education or race

or looks,

hold me back.

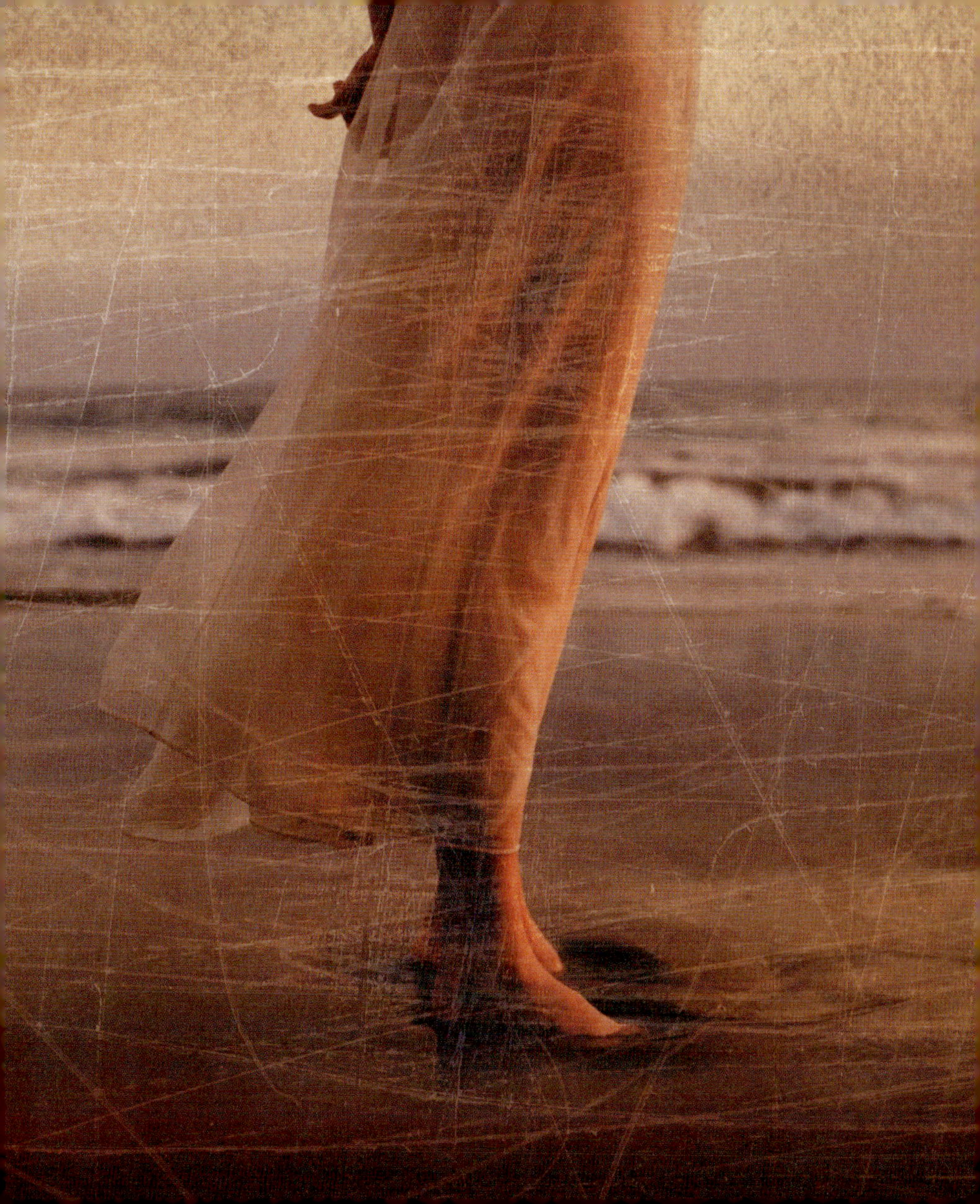

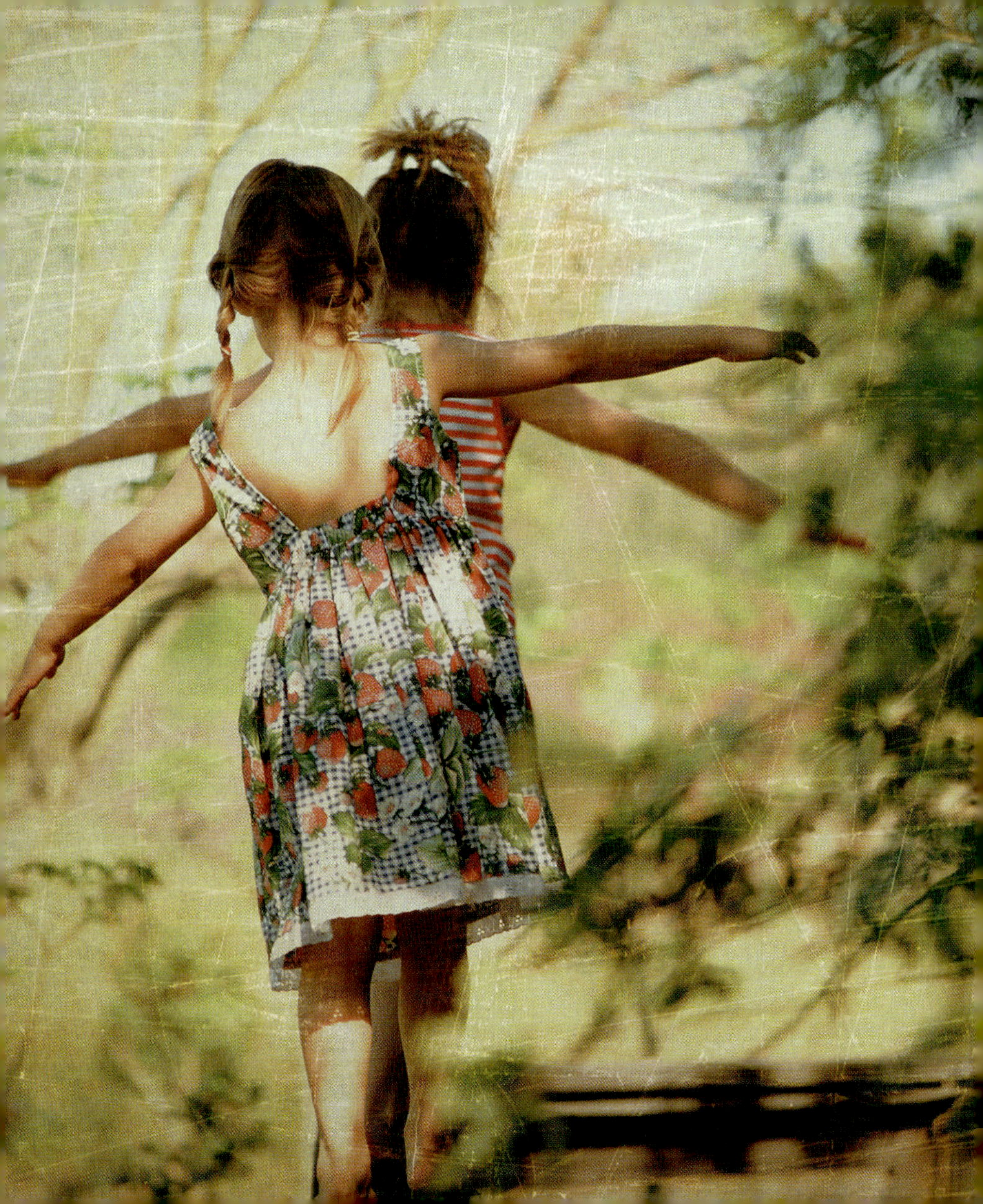

While I Still Can Dance . . .

I will delight in the sheer pleasure

of being with you . . .

just being with you.

Days spent with you

are among the best in my world.

TO DANCE . . .

I will establish

moral boundaries to live by

and refuse to compromise them . . .

for anyone or anything.

DANCE WHILE YOU CAN . . .

I will stop chasing after happiness

as though it is something

I can obtain from outside myself.

I will choose to be happy on the inside

and give joy to others.

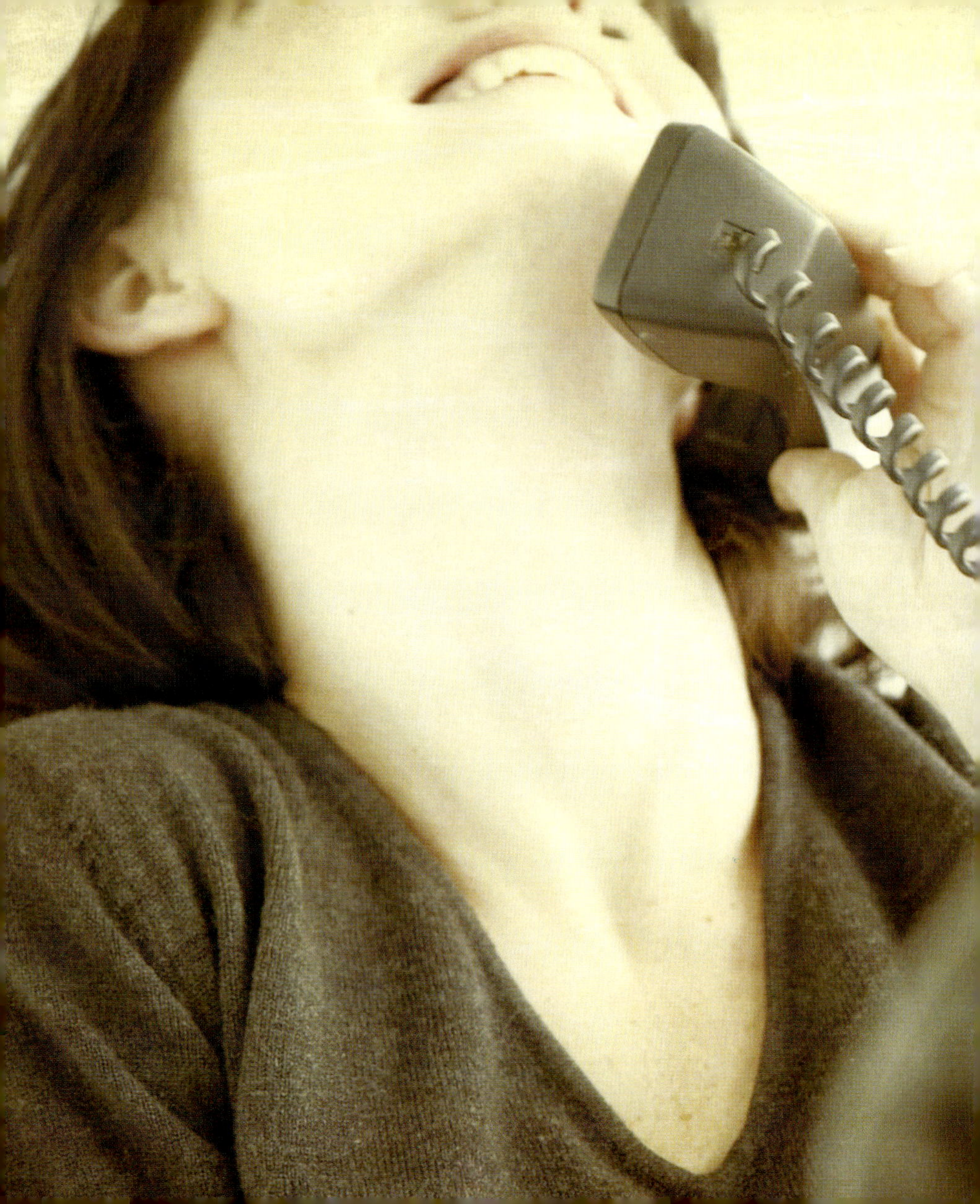

While I Still Can Dance . . .

I will cherish your every word . . .

the sound and inflections of your voice . . .

with all my heart.

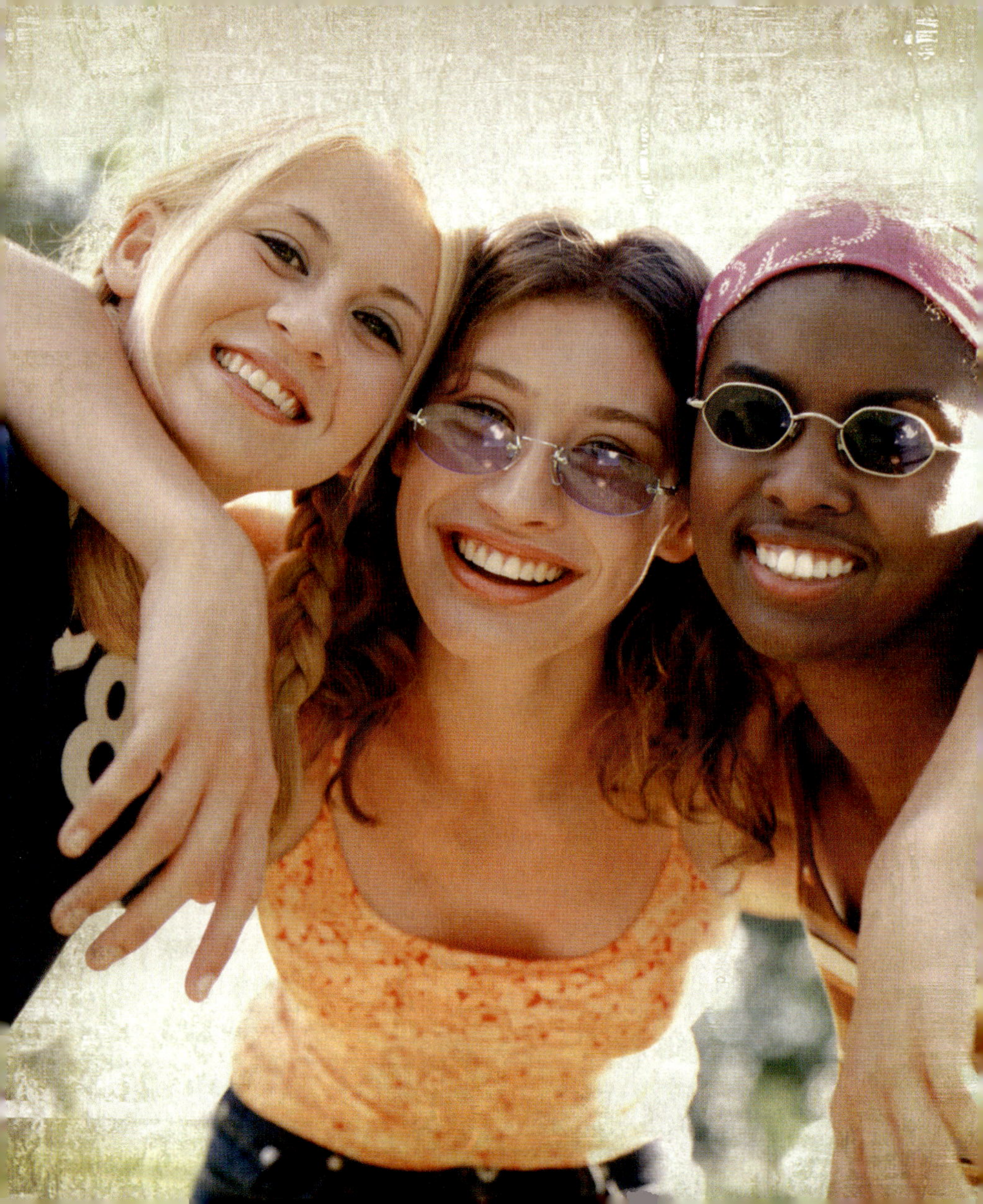

TO DANCE . . .

I will make the necessary changes in my life

to ensure that I am truly living consistently

with what I want to be in my heart

and what I say I believe in.

I will remember that money is only material,

that titles and positions mean little,

but that who I am is what really matters.

Dance While You Can . . .

I will take time for God,

to read His Word,

to seek His direction for my life.

He is the Lord of the Dance.

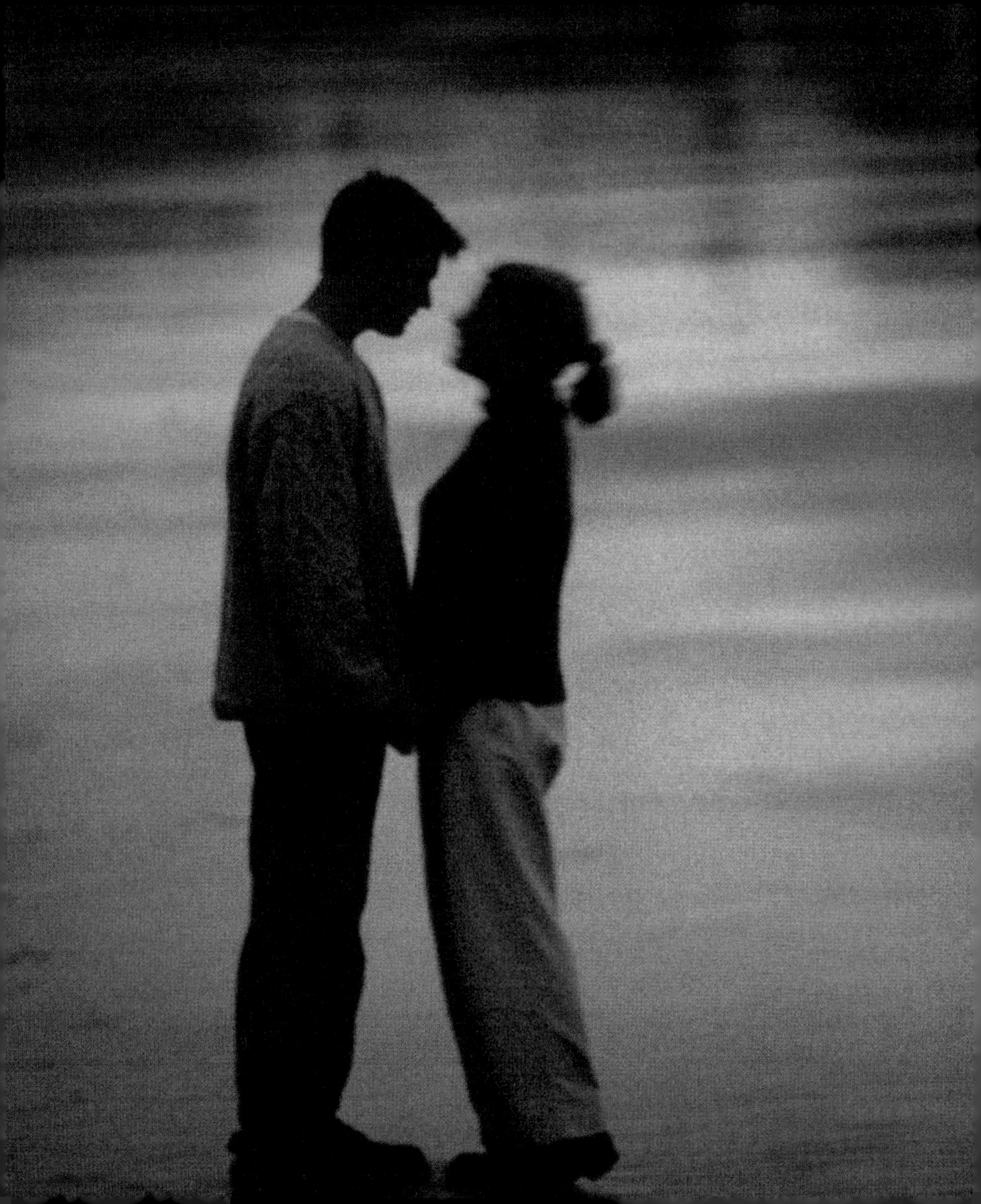

While I Still Can Dance . . .

I will let your smile drive the dark away,
your voice still my storms,
and your hugs charm my fears away.

To Dance . . .

    I will measure my words ever so carefully

        and make certain I speak the truth in love.

    I will suppress the urge to win arguments

        and prove I'm right.

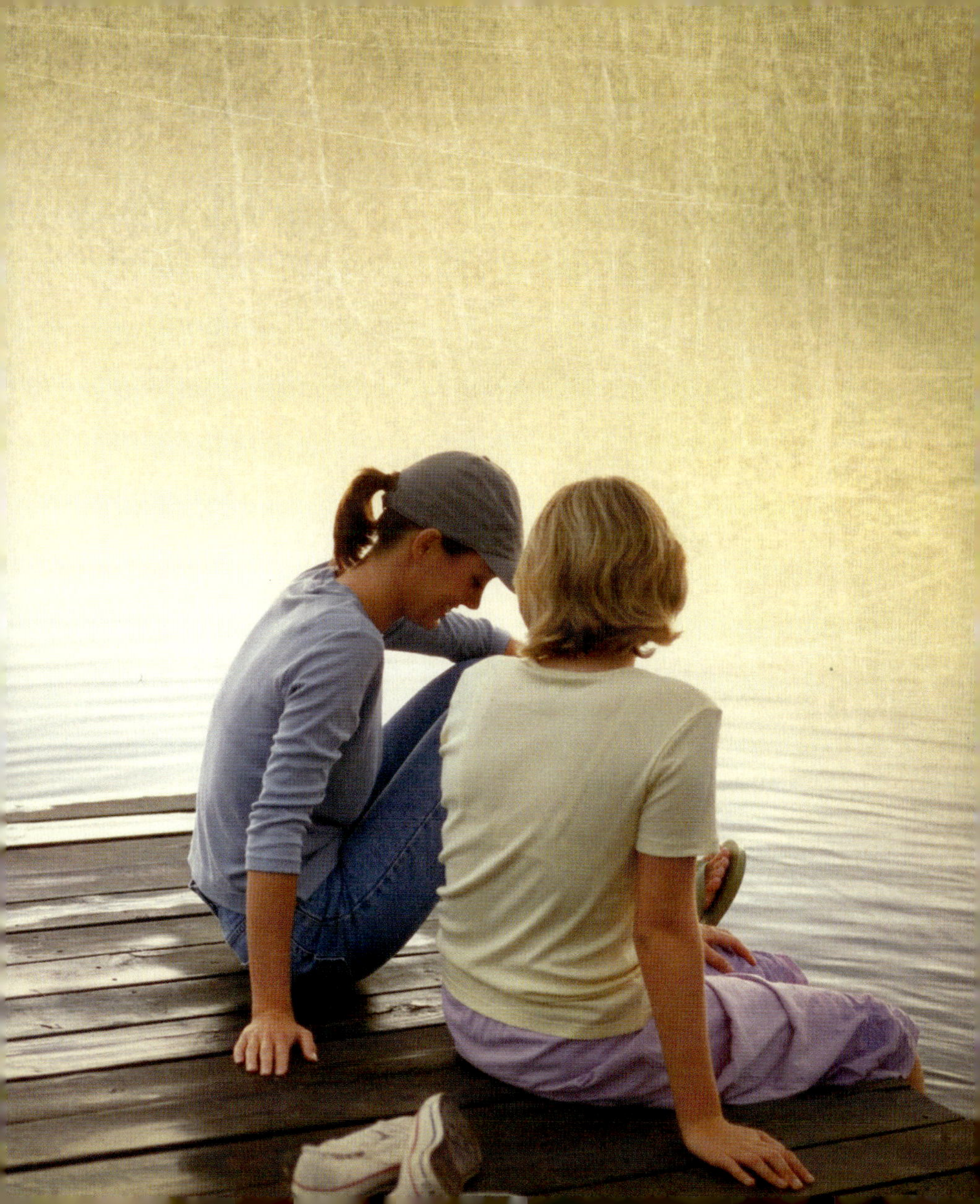

DANCE WHILE YOU CAN . . .

I will stop hiding my problems

and doubts and trepidation

and confront whatever is in front of me

in the present moment.

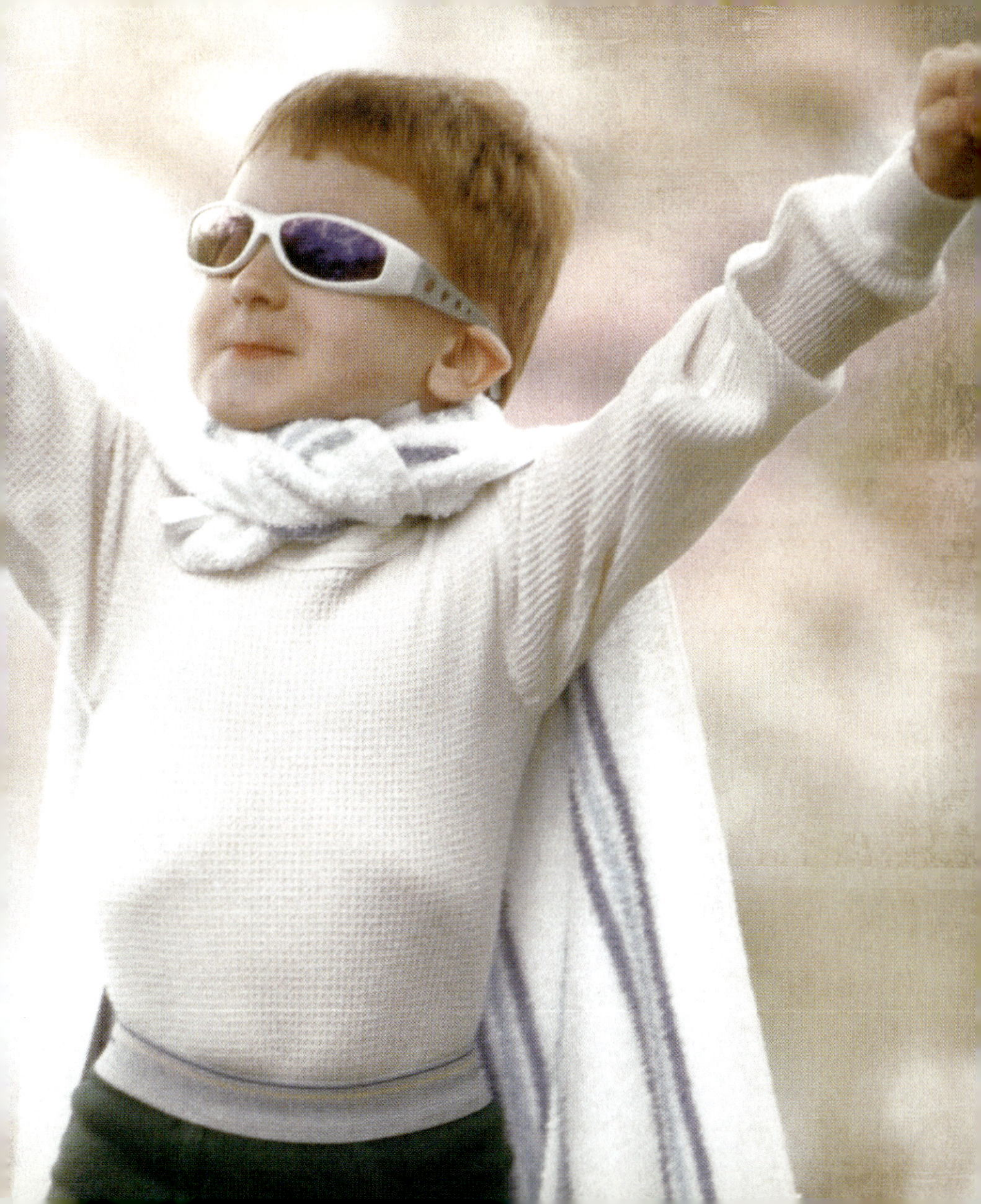

While I Still Can Dance . . .

I hope you know

that in my heart and dreams

nothing will ever change my love for you.

What I feel for you is eternal.

To Dance...

I will do all that I can,

with whatever I have,

wherever I am...

and I'll let good enough

be good enough.